D0331768

Also available:

The Not-so-Little Princess:

What's My Name?
Best Friends!
Where's Gilbert?

The Not-so-Little Princess

COLOUR READER

Spooky Night!

Wendy Finney
Tony Ross

ANDERSEN PRESS

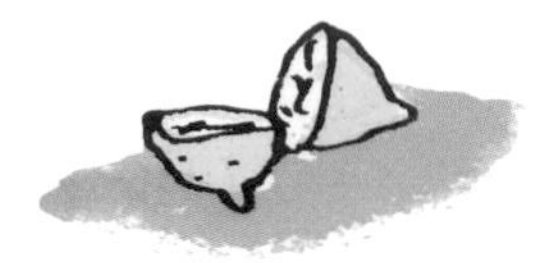

First published in 2017 by
Andersen Press Limited
20 Vauxhall Bridge Road
London SW1V 2SA
www.andersenpress.co.uk

2 4 6 8 10 9 7 5 3 1

British Library Cataloguing in Publication Data available.

ISBN 978 1 78344 383 3

Printed and bound in Malaysia by Tien Wah Press

Contents

Chapter 1

It was the middle of the night, when everyone in the castle was asleep (except for the mice). Princess Rosie was in her bed, dreaming of sweets, holidays and jam tarts.

Suddenly, she sat up and rubbed her eyes. All around was dark. Something had just woken her from a deep sleep – she had heard a noise!

She strained her ears to listen, and there it was again – a strange sound coming from above.

WOOOOOOOO . . . PARP!
WOOOOOOO . . . PARP!

That was the most awful thing she had ever heard in her life!

She hid under her bedclothes, shivering in fright . . . What on earth could it be?

Then there it was a third time!

WOOOOO . . . PARP!
WOOOOO . . . PARP!

The next morning Rosie was STILL under the duvet with her pillow clamped round her ears, thinking about the strange noise.

She felt something lift the end of her bedclothes and her brother Prince Billy's face grinned at her from under the sheets!

"Why are you hiding under your bedclothes?" he said, looking curious.

"Well, why are YOU scrabbling about at the end of MY bed? What are you doing? You scared me to death!"

Billy looked pleadingly at his big sister. "Sorry, but I am looking for my hamsters! They got out of their cage. Have you seen them?"

"No, I haven't! And I jolly well hope they aren't in MY bed," she said, wriggling her toes. "Go and ask Maidy to help . . . she knows all the nooks and crannies in the castle."

"Ta, sis!" Prince Billy seemed happy with this answer and scooted off to find Maidy.

Rosie decided not to tell anyone about the strange noise except her all-time best friend, Ollie, who shared all her secrets.

Later on that morning, the sun shone down brightly and, sure enough, Ollie ambled up the driveway towards the big front doors of the castle. The two friends had decided to spend the day together making up games and getting into mischief.

To Ollie's surprise, Rosie came running out and grabbed him.

She wanted to tell him something secret.

"What's up, old bean?" he said, lifting up his specs to see her face more clearly.

"I heard a strange WOOOOOOO! sound in the middle of the night," she said excitedly, her eyes growing large.

"What sort of a WOOOOOO?" he asked.

"What do you mean, 'What sort of WOOOOOO?'" She was looking a bit cross at this silly question.

Ollie explained himself. “Because – if it has a ‘TWIT’ in front of it then it could have been an owl! TWIT-TWOOO!”

“No, it was just an ordinary WOOOOOOO!” she retorted. “So it wasn’t an owl. All I know is it scared the living daylights out of me!”

She suddenly looked thoughtful.

"Mind you – it did end with a raspberry, like this!" And she blew a long raspberry with her tongue. "It went sort of WOOOOOOOOO . . . PARP!"

Ollie looked excited.

"WOOOOOO . . . PARP, indeed! In the middle of the night! What could it be?" He ran round in circles blowing raspberries and being silly.

"My word . . . a marvellous mystery – just what we need to add a bit of excitement to the school holidays!"

Off the friends went to their favourite place down in the fruit patch to plan what to do about it all.

Chapter 2

"This is very peculiar," said Ollie when they were sitting among the raspberry canes. "What do you think the spooky noise is?"

"I don't know," said Rosie. "It will probably be a monster . . . I bet it is big, green and scaly with huge pointed teeth, horns, red glowing eyes and breath that could melt a bus . . . "

Then she added, "Actually, it sounded like an elephant with a cold."

Ollie looked at his pal.

"Do you know what an elephant with a cold sounds like?"

"No, of course not!" she said.

"But I have an IMAGINATION . . . that I use to IMAGINE what things are like . . ."

"Oh, I see," said Ollie, but he had a look on his face that showed he didn't really know what she was going on about.

"Well, anyway – this calls for an investigation by the Deadly Detectives," Rosie declared, holding up her finger. "Or maybe, the Cracking Crime-Crunchers."

"Who are they?" said Ollie.

"Why, you and me of course," said Rosie. "We are going to find out what is happening . . . and it will have to be done after dark when the WOOOOOO monster is about . . . Are you up for it, Ollie?"

"Ooh-er . . . erm . . . yes, I suppose so," he said, sounding unsure.

Later that day, Rosie and Ollie were in the big castle kitchen having lemony pancakes for supper. Maidy was busy making a batch of her famous jam tarts.

Ollie was allowed to stay the night, which was useful as they had planned to find out what the WOOOOOOO noise was.

"Can Ollie sleep in my room?" Rosie asked.

"No – it isn't the done thing!" said Maidy firmly.

"Why not?" exclaimed Rosie. "I can make it the done thing cos I am a princess and I can do as I like!" She looked hard at Maidy as if to say, *Give me a good answer to that!* "AND . . . he can sleep in the dog basket!" added Rosie.

"I DON'T WANT TO SLEEP IN THE DOG BASKET – IT PONGS!" Ollie said loudly.

Scruff the dog woofed at this insult and slunk off to the throne room to gnaw his bone.

"Definitely NOT!" said Maidy and she marched Ollie off to the guest bedroom on the other side of the castle.

Chapter 3

Much later, in the dead of night, Rosie was snoring loudly in her bed. Ollie tapped quietly on her bedroom door.

He put his ear to the door panel. *What a racket*, he thought, listening to her snores. He tried knocking a bit louder.

Eventually she woke up and sleepily opened the door.

"What do you want? Don't let Mum and Dad hear or they will come steaming in and not let you stay any more," she hissed.

"Have you forgotten already? We are going to investigate the WOOOOOOO . . . PARP thing," said Ollie. "You know, the noise *you* heard in the middle of the night."

"Oh yes, the THING," said Rosie, yawning. "Do we HAVE to? I am SO sleepy."

"Yes, we DO. I haven't got all dressed up like this for nothing!" Ollie looked down at himself.

"Why *are* you dressed like that?" Rosie grinned, rubbing the sleep out of her eyes and looking her friend up and down.

Ollie was all in black, with a black bobble hat on his head and his large glasses plonked back on over it.

"Cos I don't want to be seen in the dark. You should do the same. The thing must not be able to see us. And we also have to be quiet, as good detectives should. Go and find something black to wear, and hurry up."

Rosie toddled off back into her bedroom and started scrabbling around looking for stuff.

She came back wearing a large black bin bag with long black socks, black gloves and black wellingtons.

"Now we had better get a move on!" said Ollie. "You first, as you know your way round the castle."

Chapter 4

The friends made their way along the dark corridor outside Rosie's bedroom, trying not to creak on the floorboards too much.

They went past Prince Billy's bedroom door. He was wide awake and dressed because he was still looking for his missing pets.

Now he came out to see what all the squeaky floorboard noise was, thinking the squeaks were his hamsters!

And there he saw the horrible sight of two shapes dressed all in black!

Rosie leaped forwards and clapped her hand over his mouth before he could let out a piercing scream.

"Go back to bed NOW, before the bogeyman gets you!" she whispered fiercely in his ear.

Prince Billy recognised his sister's voice. He bit her finger!

Rosie would have let out an extremely loud OOOOOWWWW! But she couldn't . . . so she tucked her fingers in her armpit and did a quiet dance on the spot!

"You little beast!" she hissed.

"What are you doing up?" asked Billy. "Why have you got black clothes on? I will tell Mum and Dad if you don't let me come . . ." He was cut short as Rosie stuffed the end of an old curtain in his mouth to try to shut him up. He squirmed to get free.

"OK! OK! OK!" she said. "You can come, but if you dare make a noise I will . . ." She didn't get to finish what she was saying, for just at that moment, they heard the muffled sound of a WOOOOOOOOOO . . . PARP!

“IT’S THE THING!” said Ollie.

“Here, put this over you . . . you have to be in disguise,” said Rosie. Before he could say anything more, Rosie pulled the curtain off its rail and put it over Prince Billy.

He was scared by the strange sound and clung to his big sister.

"W-w-what's that noise?" he said, his voice shaky.

"We don't know," whispered the pals together. "But we are going to find out."

Prince Billy really wanted to go back into his bedroom, push his big wardrobe against the door and carry on looking for his hamsters, but he wasn't going to let these two see he was scared, so he crept along behind them with the curtain still round him.

Off went the three, up into the darkest parts of the castle.

Chapter 5

Just at that moment the General came into the downstairs hall with Scruff the dog at his heels.

He was doing his night-time rounds to make sure all was well. Scruff was following him and generally getting in the way.

He came into the hall just in time to see the dark shapes of Rosie, Ollie and Billy creeping along the upstairs landing.

"Burglars!" he muttered to himself. Drawing his sword, he went quietly up the stairs two at a time to catch up.

He soon saw them turning the corner into the long picture gallery.

He had just gone past Maidy's bedroom door when she came out to get a bedtime cup of hot milk.

"What are you doing?" she hissed.

"Burglars!" he said, putting his fingers to his lips and pointing. "They want to steal the crown jewels!"

"And what are you going to do with that?" she asked, looking at the sword. "Cut off someone's head?"

"No, of course not, I am just going to frighten them with it . . . that's all!"

Maidy fished in her pocket for her old tape measure. "Something to tie 'em up with when we have caught 'em," she said.

And off they went together in pursuit of the dark figures, with Scruff bringing up the rear.

"WOOF!" said Scruff.

"SSSSSHHHHHH!" said the General and Maidy to the dog.

The King and Queen heard the muffled "woof" just outside their bedroom door and came out to see what was happening, yawning and stretching.

Once they learned what was going on, they joined in.

"Burglars indeed, how dare they!" said the King, pulling himself up to his full height. The King had armed himself with his old cricket bat and the Queen had quickly grabbed her knitting. She thought that the needles were nice and sharp, perfect for a weapon.

The King stared at her. "Dearest . . . why have you brought your knitting? Are you planning to make the burglars a jumper?" he said, laughing.

"Very amusing indeed!" said the Queen, giving the King a little push, and off they all went following the intruders.

Very soon they were passing the

Chef's door. They decided to wake him up to join them. He came out, armed with a great big heavy frying pan in order to clout the burglars. He always kept a frying pan under his bed just in case.

Soon the Admiral and the Doctor had joined the group tiptoeing along the dark corridors after the mystery burglars.

The Admiral had brought an old anchor from his rowing boat.

"What are you planning to do with that? It's a bit heavy, isn't it?" said the Doctor.

"I'm going to knock their jolly old blocks off!" said the Admiral, and swung the anchor through the air.

Everyone had to duck.

"Steady on, Admiral," said the King. "We will all end up in the sick bay!"

With that, off they all went, slowly following the dark shapes at a distance and trying their best not to make any noise.

The children hadn't heard all the kerfuffle going on downstairs. They were too eager to find out what the noise was. But so far they'd found nothing.

They climbed up to the attic rooms at the top of the castle, where no one usually went. It was very dark and cobwebby up there. They had to feel their way about.

WOOOOO . . . PARP!

The sound was definitely coming from somewhere up here.

"I-I-I don't like this!" said Rosie.

"N-n-neither do I!" said Ollie.

"M-m-me neither. I wish the grown-ups were here!" said Prince Billy, in a very babyish voice.

"THE GROWN-UPS *ARE* HERE!" said the King loudly. He suddenly appeared from the dark, whisked a torch out of his pocket, and shone it in Princess Rosie's face, giving her a terrible fright!

Chapter 6

"What on earth are you doing? And why are you dressed like burglars?" asked the King when they had all calmed down.

"We thought you were coming to steal the crown jewels," declared the General, putting his sword away.

"Yes, you nearly got your blocks knocked off," said the Admiral, swinging the anchor.

Before the children could answer, there was another very loud

WOOOOOO . . . PARP!

Then they heard someone muttering behind one of the attic doors.

"Bother and blow! This old thing . . . I am going to jolly well get myself a new one!"

"That's the Prime Minister's voice – what's he doing up here?" said the Queen, going through the door.

Everyone followed the Queen.

There was the Prime Minister, holding a great big battered brass musical instrument. He was blowing down it as hard as he could to try and get a tune out of it.

He stopped blowing and looked sheepishly at everyone. "Oh dear . . . I seem to have woken the whole castle . . . "

"You were making such horrible noises, we thought you were a monster with green scales!" said Rosie, and the children crowded round the Prime Minister.

"I am SO sorry!" he said apologetically. "I have joined the brass band in the town and I merely wanted to practise on my old tuba. I didn't want to make a horrible racket and annoy everyone so thought if I hid away up here in the dead of night, I wouldn't disturb anybody. Only problem is, there's something wrong with it and I can't get a tune out of it any more."

He looked down sadly at his old musical instrument.

"What do you think is wrong?" asked Rosie, stepping forward and taking the heavy tuba.

"It sounds terrible!" laughed Prince Billy. "Like there is something stuck in it!"

Rosie carefully put in her hand and felt around inside.

"LOOK! THERE *IS* SOMETHING STUCK IN IT!" exclaimed Rosie in surprise.

Everyone crowded round to look inside the horn of the instrument and they all gasped in amazement and delight as she showed them what she'd found.

"MY HAMSTERS! Harry and Harriet!" Billy squealed. "They've made a nest in there AND they have had lots of little babies!"

Sure enough, there were Mum and Dad hamster, looking up proudly, surrounded by lots of little squiggly, brown bundles of fur.

"AAAAAAHHHHHHHHHHH! HOW SWEEEEEEEEEEEEEET!" said everyone.

"Well," said Rosie, looking down at the hamsters happily making their nest. "I think that as they like living inside the tuba, they should stay where they are!"

"A splendid idea, young lady," said the King. "And we will get the Prime Minister a brand new tuba so he can play in the band."

"What a good plan!" said everyone.

Then they all started yawning.

"Enough excitement for one night," proclaimed Maidy. She knew when to be bossy! "Back to bed everybody! That means you two as well," she said, looking at the King and Queen.

They all knew not to disobey Maidy, so off they went, back to bed.

Prince Billy carried his hamsters in the tuba down to his bedroom and put it in pride of place at the end of his bed.

"How many more super adventures are we going to have?" exclaimed Ollie.

"You two can stop nattering and go to bed as well," Maidy said, looking sharply at Rosie and Ollie. "AND maybe, just *maybe*, you can have jam tarts for breakfast!"

"Jam tarts for breakfast instead of mouldy old porridge. YIPPEE!" shouted Rosie. "AND . . . we found Billy's hamsters! All thanks to the Cracking Crime-Crunching Deadly Detectives!"

"Who are they?" said Maidy.

"Why, US OF COURSE!" shouted Rosie and Ollie together.

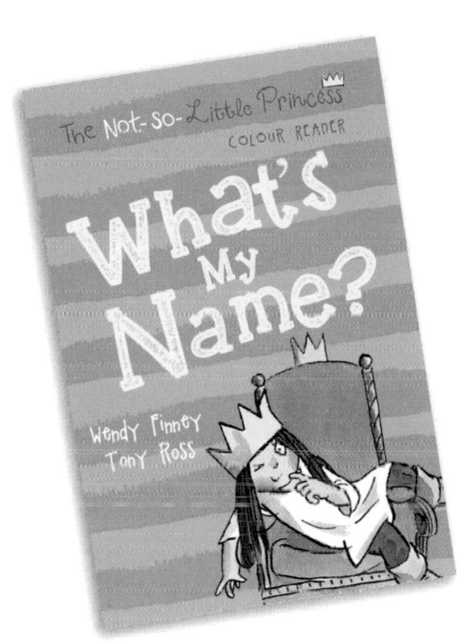

The Little Princess

is not so little any more!

Now that she's growing up, people can't keep calling her the LITTLE Princess. But her real name is **horrible** and no one dares tell her what it is!

What will the Not-so-Little Princess do when she finds out?

The Little Princess has got a brand new friend!

The Princess's new friend Ollie is different in every way - from his funny old-fashioned voice to his odd clothes.

And when they go exploring, there's a BIG surprise in store for them ...